KU-661-476

WITHDRAWN
FROM
STOCK

# Digger Dog

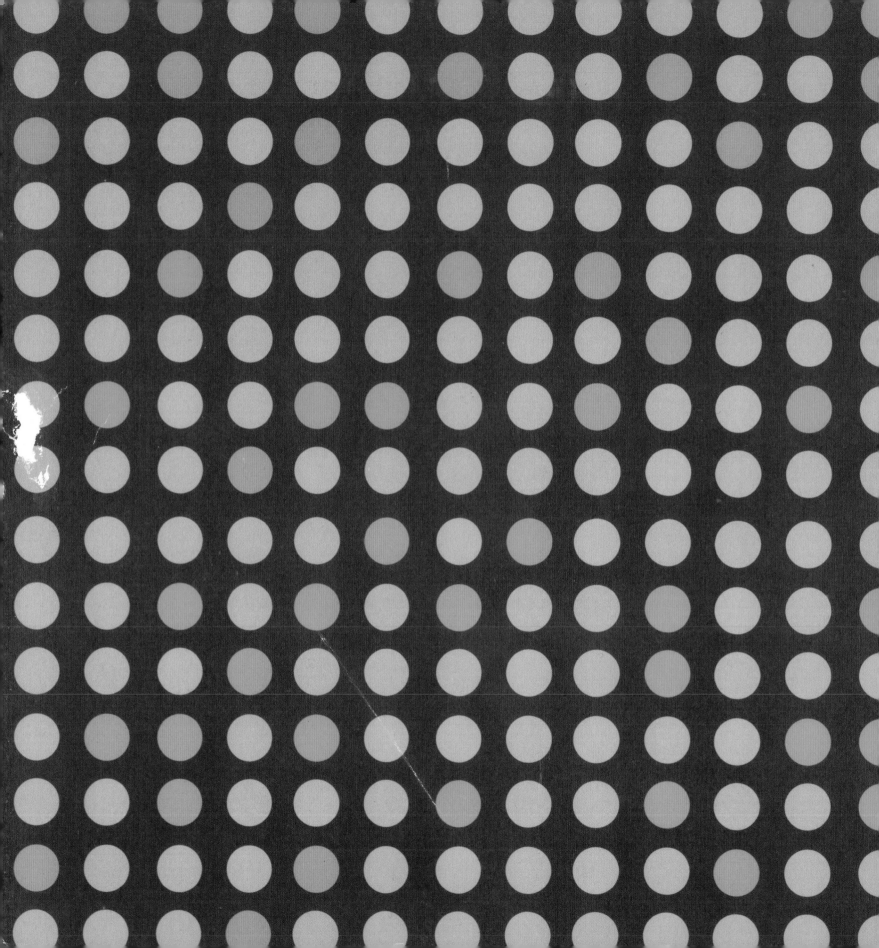

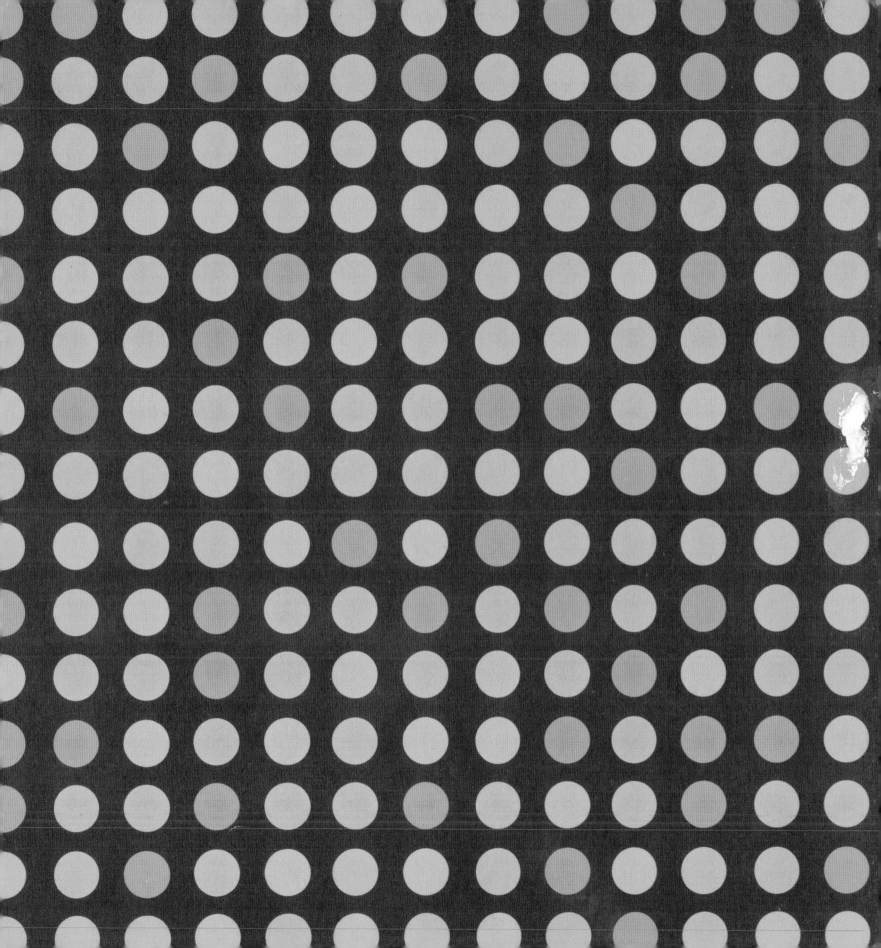

# For Ulf, with love C.J.

First published in 2013 by Nosy Crow Ltd

The Crow's Nest, 10a Lant Street

London SE1 1QR

www.nosycrow.com

ISBN 978 0 85763 128 2 (HB)

ISBN 978 0 85763 129 9 (PB)

Nosy Crow and associated logos are trademarks and /or registered trademarks
of Nosy Crow Ltd.

Text © William Bee 2013

Illustrations © Cecilia Johansson 2013

The right of William Bee to be identified as the author
and Cecilia Johansson as the illustrator of this work has been asserted.

All rights reserved.

This book is sold subject to the condition that it shall not, by way of trade
or otherwise, be lent, hired out or otherwise circulated in any form of binding
or cover other than that in which it is published. No part of this publication
may be reproduced, stored in a retrieval system, or transmitted in any
form or by any means (electronic, mechanical, photocopying,
recording or otherwise) without the prior written
permission of Nosy Crow Ltd.

A CIP catalogue record for this book is available
from the British Library.

Printed in China

5 7 9 8 6 4

# Digger Dog

**Illustrated by Cecilia Johansson**
**Written by William Bee**

nosy crow

# This is **Digger Dog**.

**Digger Dog** loves to **dig**.

And he especially loves to **dig** for bones.

He finds them with his **great big**

**nose!**

Sniff, sniff, sniff, sniff, sniff.

Digger Dog's got the scent of something . . .

. . . something **BIG.**
So **Digger Dog** starts to **dig.**

**Dig, dig,
dig,
dig,
dig.**

**But the ground is too hard and the bone is too deep.**

**So Digger Dog**
goes and gets . . .

...**a little digger** so he can **dig** deeper and quicker.

**Dig, dig, dig, dig, dig.**

But the ground is still
**too hard**
and the bone is still
**too deep.**

So **Digger Dog**
goes and gets . . .

. . . a bigger digger
so he can **dig** deeper
and quicker.

**Dig, dig,
dig,
dig,
dig.**

But the ground is **still too hard** and the bone is **still too deep.**

So **Digger Dog** goes and gets . . .

. . . a much bigger digger
so he can **dig** deeper and quicker.

**Dig, dig, dig, dig, dig.**

But the ground is **still too hard** and the bone is **still too deep.**

Oh dear, will **Digger Dog** ever
reach that **big, big bone?**

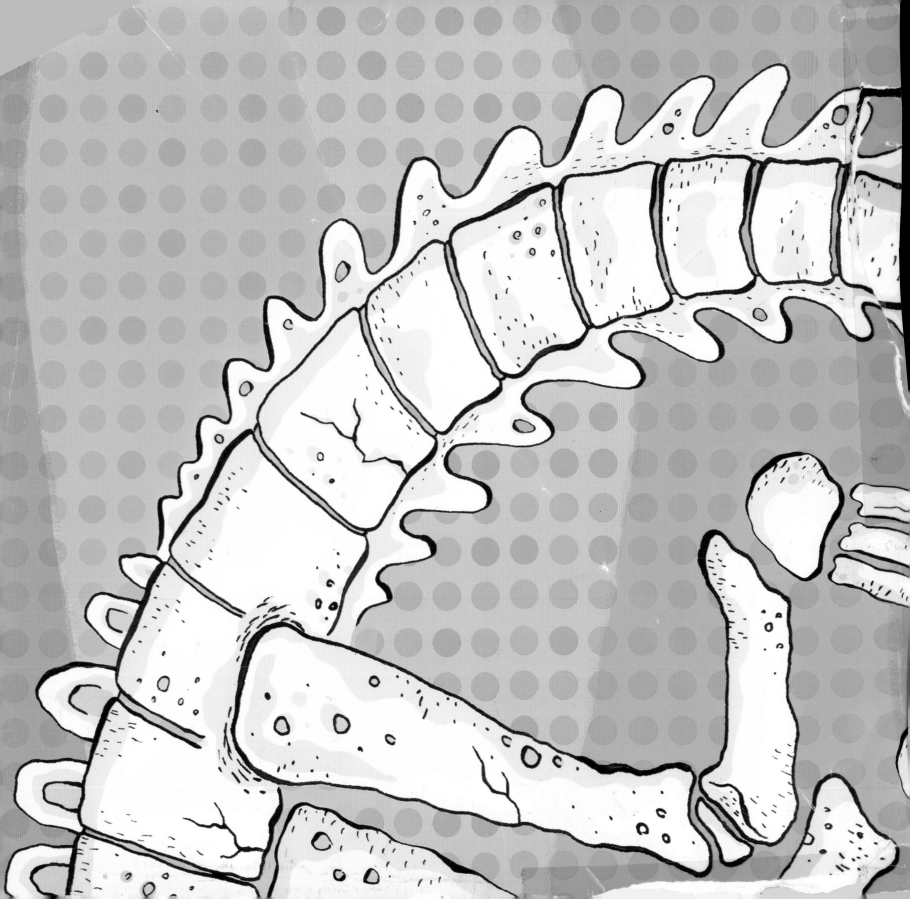

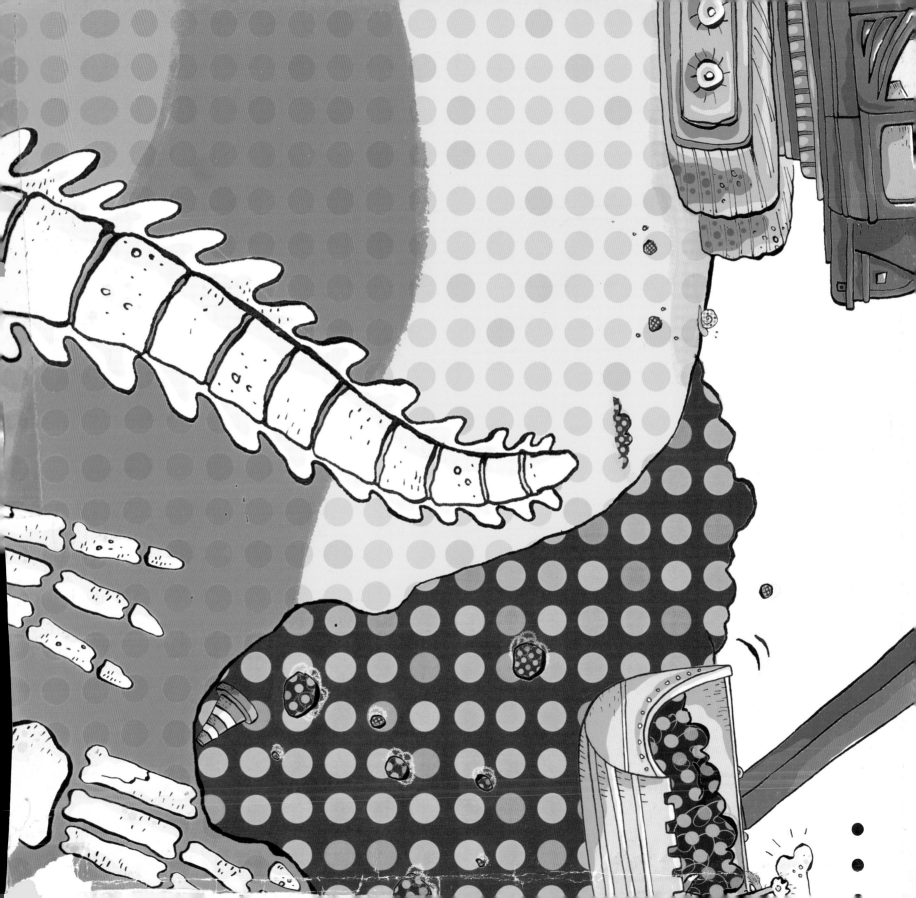

. . . . the world's **biggest digger digs up** the world's . . . .

TURN PAGE

**Digger Dog** goes and gets . . .

. . . **spits** and
**snorts** and
**rumbles** and **shakes**
and **digs!**

# Dig! Dig! Dig! Dig! Dig!

And sure enough,
after a lot of
**digging** . . .

# The
# biggest digger
### in
### the . . .

And the biggest digger
in the whole world . . .

...whole
world!

... the
# biggest digger
### he
### can
### find.

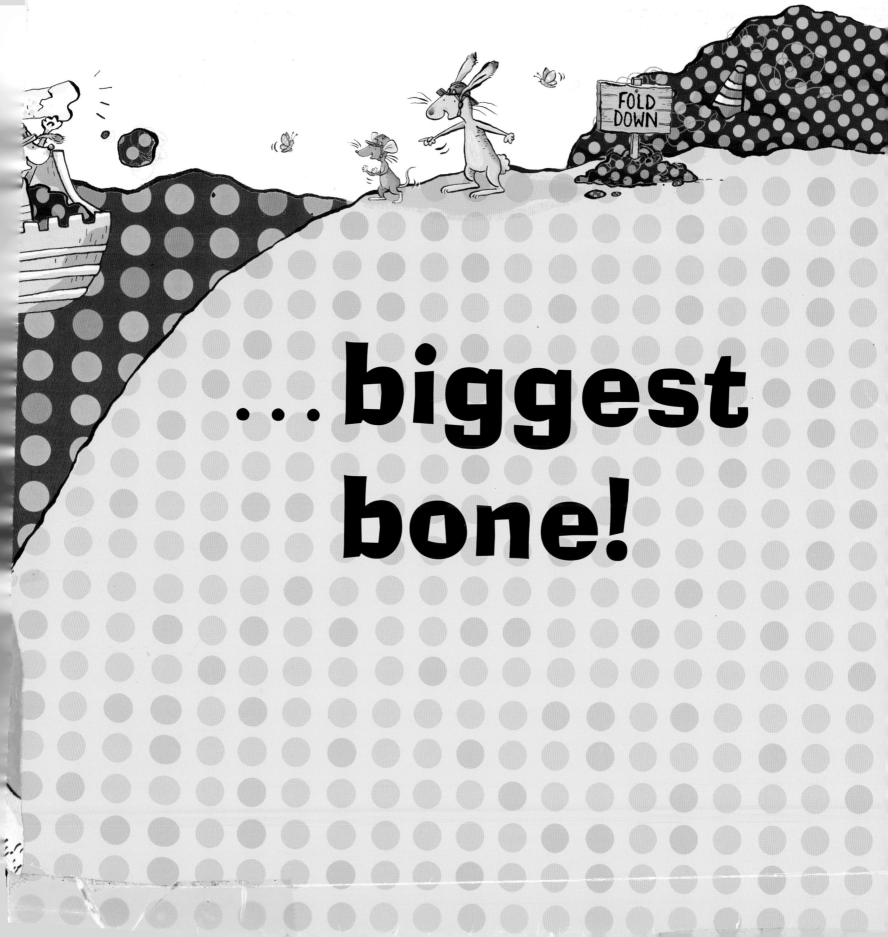

... biggest
bone!

FOLD
DOWN

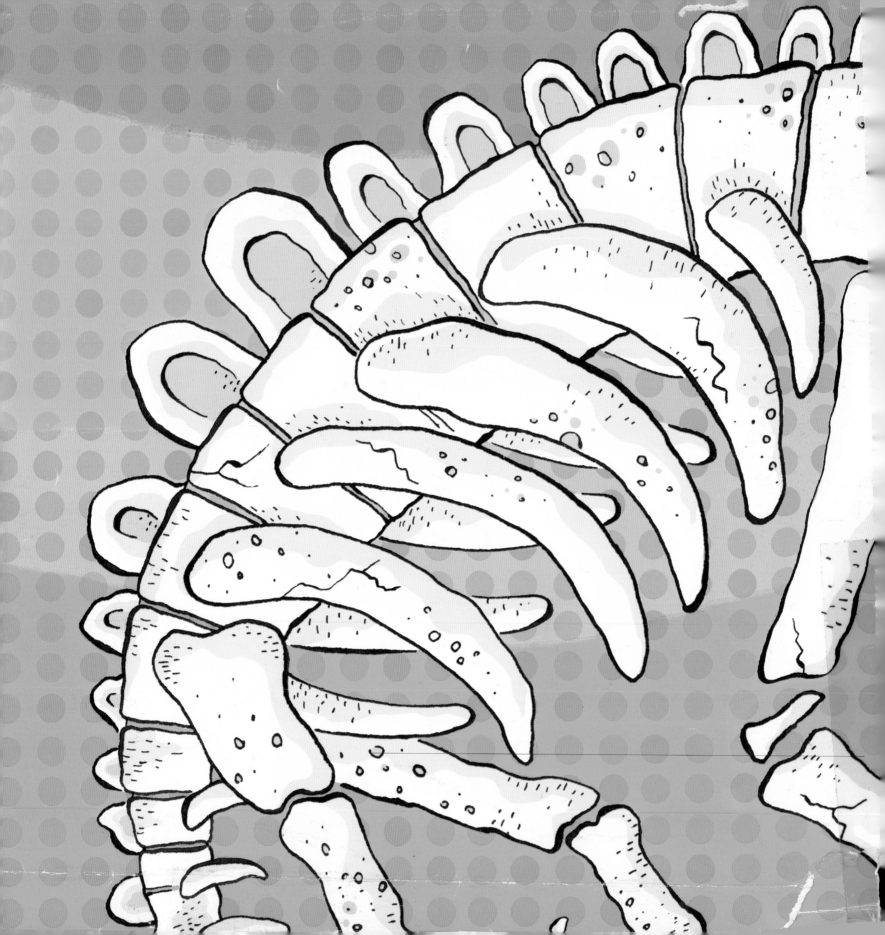